The Land of Shapes

Volume 2:

Cooking with Pierre and Square

Sugar Cookies

The Land of Shapes Vol. 2: Cooking with Pierre and Square Sugar Cookies
Copyright © 2013 by Colin McConnell. All rights reserved.
First Print Edition: November 2013

This book is best suited for children between the age of 2 and 10, but can still be enjoyed by someone of any age.

COOKING WITH

Pierre
and
Square

Episode 1: Sugar Cookies

by: Colin McConnell

Square

Square

Welcome to the Cooking with Pierre and Square TV show.

What are they cooking up today?
Let's find out!
Here are your hosts,
Pierre and Square.

"Today my friend Square
and I are making our famous
sugar cookies." said Pierre.

"My favorite part about making sugar cookies, is to cut them into fun shapes and decorating them."

"My favorite part is eating them!" Square said excitedly. "The most important thing about cooking is having a grown up with you," Pierre said. "Now we are going to need a BIG mixing bowl," said Square.

"In the mixing bowl we are going to add 1/3 cup sugar and 1/3 cup butter," Pierre said while pouring the sugar and butter into the big bowl.

"Mix the ingredients on low, with an electric mixer, for 30 seconds." Square said.

Pierre then told the audience to add 1 cup of flour, ¾ cups sugar, 1 tablespoon of milk, 1 teaspoon of baking powder, 1 teaspoon of vanilla, a pinch of salt...

...and one egg.
"Hey! That egg looks like my friend Oval!"
Square said with a smile on his face.

"Get another cup of flour, but keep it next to you, just for a little bit." Square explained. "Now, stir the ingredients together. While slowly stirring the ingredients, slowly add the flour to the bowl."

"Once all the ingredients are combined, split them into two balls, cover them, and put them in the refrigerator for 3 hours, or until the dough is easy to handle," Square said.

"When it is easy to handle,
have the grown up pre heat
the oven to 375 degrees."

"Roll out the dough on a floured surface 1/4 to 1/2 inch thick. Cut into shapes with any cookie cutter you desire. Place cookies 1 inch apart on an ungreased cookie sheet." explained Pierre. "We made ours into Circles and Stars," Square said

"Once the shapes are cut, place them on the cookie sheet 1 inch apart. Then, let the grown up put them in the oven for 7-8 minutes, or once the bottom of the cookies are a very light brown," said Square.

"Once the cookies are cool, you
can decorate them however
you want," said Pierre.
"Here are some we did earlier."

Now for Square's favorite part ... eating the cookies.

**Thanks for watching Cooking
with Pierre and Square.
We hope you had fun.**

Till next time...
Happy Cooking!

Activities with Square

Place your finger on Square and
slowly trace the dotted lines.
Try and trace Square four times.

10 reasons to cook with your child

1. Boosting their self confidence. Seeing the end result of what they made is a great opportunity to gain a sense of accomplishment. Make sure to let everyone know who the chef was. "Ella's cookies" or "Gavin's Pizza."

2. Cooking helps build math skills. From counting how many eggs to pouring in a ½ a cup of flour.

3. Cooking together reduces the number of meals eaten outside the home.

4. It encourages kids to try new foods.

5. Spending quality time will help build memories and tradition that they will pass on with their kids.

6. Kids aren't spending time in front of the TV or computer while they're cooking.

7. Learning to cook is a skill your children can use for the rest of their lives.

8. By reading the recipe together and aloud, you're introducing new words to your child's vocabulary and promoting literacy.

9. Following steps in the recipe can work on listening skills.

10. Fun for all the senses. Pounding the dough, smelling the ingredients and tasting the final masterpiece are just a couple things that your child will experience.

Place your finger on the dotted line.

Help Pierre get to Square,

put the cookies in the oven,

and get Oval to the egg.

If you enjoyed this story, be sure to check out the next installment in the Land of the Shapes series:

The Land of
Shapes
Vol. 3:

Rectangle Needs
a New TV

by: Colin McConnell

Made in the USA
Monee, IL
13 May 2022